Animals that Live Under the Ground

Debbie Croft

Contents

Homes Under the Ground

There are lots of animals
that live under the ground.

Some animals hide in burrows
to be safe from bigger animals.

Some animals live in muddy holes
to stay wet and keep cool.

Some other animals live in tunnels
under the ground all their lives.

Rabbits

Rabbits live in places
where there is a lot of grass to eat.

They dig burrows
near bushes, trees or tall grass.
They dig burrows in sandy places, too.

Rabbits hide from other animals
in their burrows.

The mother rabbit makes a nest
for her babies in the **burrow**.
She puts some **straw** or grass in the nest.
She puts some of her **fur** in the nest, too.

The straw and fur
help to keep her babies warm.

Frogs

Some frogs live under the ground
when it is very hot and dry.
They can live there for years and years.

These frogs dig down in the mud to stay wet and keep cool. They only come out of their holes after it has rained for a long time.

The frogs lay their eggs
in big puddles of water.
The eggs soon turn into tadpoles
because the water is so warm.

Then the tadpoles turn into little frogs.

The frogs have to dig holes in the mud again before the ground dries out.

Earthworms

Earthworms live under the ground.
They make tunnels in the **soil**.

Earthworms are long and thin.
This helps them to move
along the tunnels.

Earthworms find food under the ground.
They eat leaves and dead plants
in the soil.

Ground Squirrels

Ground squirrels sleep in a burrow
to stay warm in winter.
They put leaves and plants
in the burrow to eat.

Mother squirrels
have their babies in the burrow, too.

Ground squirrels live in their burrows
for a long time.
They make them bigger and bigger each year.

There are lots of other animals
that live under the ground.

Glossary

burrow a hole
made in the ground
by an animal

fur soft, thick hair of animals

soil dirt and tiny stones

straw dry grass or wheat